W9-BOO-984
3 1668 07092 3112

Wisdom Tales is an imprint of World Wisdom, Inc.

Library of Congress Cataloging-in-Publication Data

Names: Jacobs, Kim, 1955- author, illustrator. | Grimm, Jacob, 1785-1863. | Grimm, Wilhelm, 1786-1859.
Title: Princess Sophie and the six swans : a tale from the Brothers Grimm / retold & illustrated by Kim Jacobs.
Other titles: Six swans. English.
Description: Bloomington, Indiana : Wisdom Tales, [2017] | Summary: A king's daughter undertakes a difficult task to rescue her six brothers from the enchantment imposed on them by their wicked stepmother.
Identifiers: LCCN 2016045888 (print) | LCCN 2016051492 (ebook) | ISBN 9781937786670 (casebound : alk. paper) | ISBN 9781937786687 (epub)
Subjects: | CYAC: Fairy tales. | Folklore--Germany.
Classification: LCC PZ8.J193 Pr 2017 (print) | LCC PZ8.J193 (ebook) | DDC 398.2 [E] --dc23
LC record available at https://lccn.loc.gov/2016045888

Printed in China on acid-free paper.
Production Date: November 2017,
Plant & Location: Printed by 1010 Printing International,
Job/Batch #: TT16100743

For information address Wisdom Tales,
P.O. Box 2682, Bloomington,
Indiana 47402-2682
www.wisdomtalespress.com

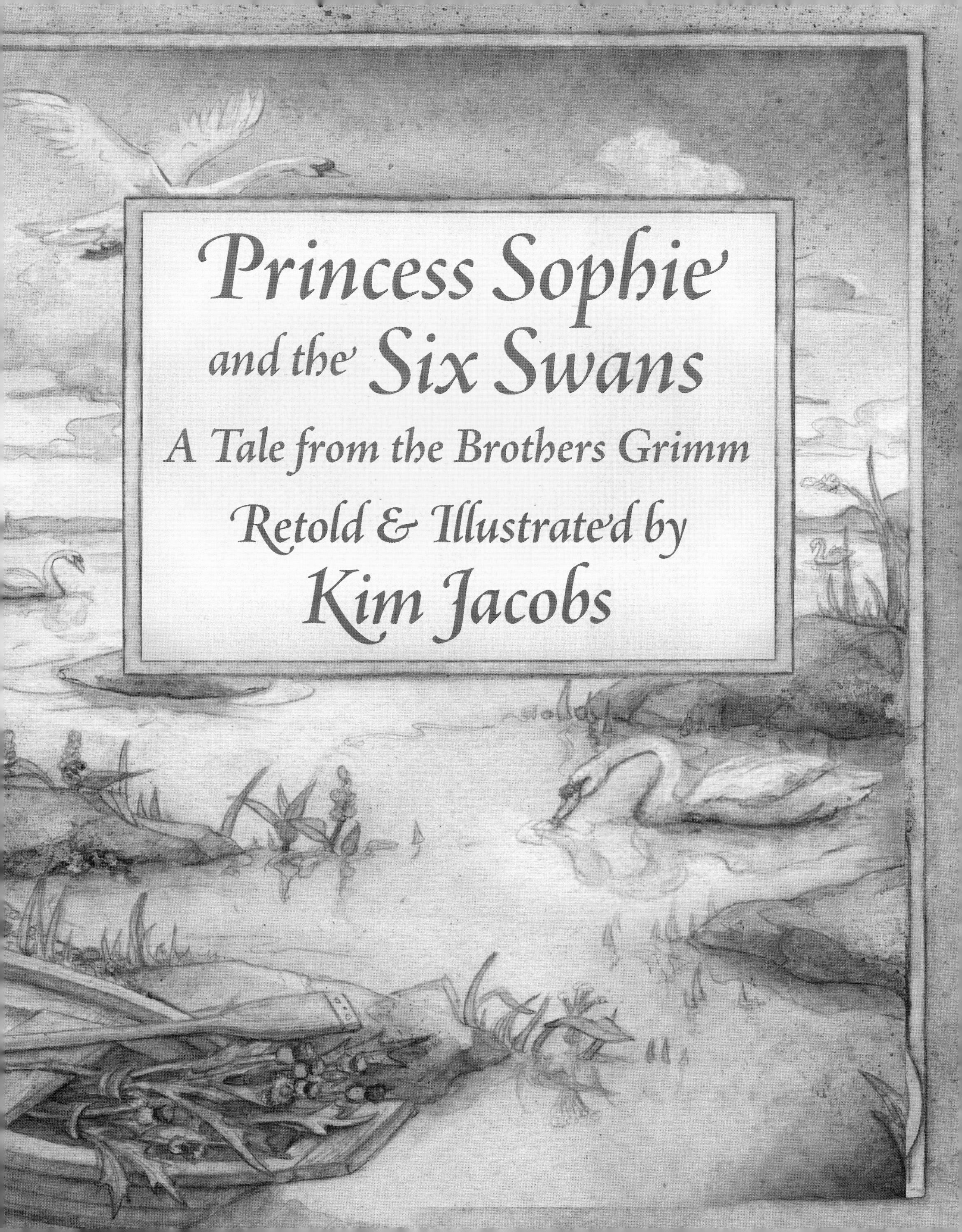
Princess Sophie
and the Six Swans
A Tale from the Brothers Grimm
Retold & Illustrated by
Kim Jacobs

When I was a child, my mother and I fed the royal swans every morning. One day she turned to me and smiled, "Know, my darling, that you are Princess Sophie of the Swans. You are loyal and strong like these noble birds, but sometimes you hide your gentle heart. Remember, be strong but also kind."

O*ur castle home* was a happy one. My brothers and I climbed and chased, tumbled and teased. The halls rang with our laughter.

Suddenly, everything changed.
My mother fell ill and died. In his sorrow, my father grew distant. We knew he still loved us, but now he hardly noticed we were there. My brothers wept. Chin up, I stomped about pretending to be brave.

Father began to wander through the castle and beyond. One day he didn't come home. We feared he was gone forever. At last he returned, but with a mysterious new wife. She had lived deep in the enchanted forest. Villagers whispered of her strange powers. Father had stumbled through her door lost and heartsick. She had cared for him and guided him home.

We ran to Father. He held us close. Our new stepmother stood by, watching. My welcoming brothers brought her flowers. “How dare she take my mother’s place!” I grumbled.

At first she ignored my resentment. With bitter, whispered words, I tried to turn Father against her. He spied a flash of anger in her eyes and feared for me.

Secretly, he brought us to a distant castle, visiting us whenever he could slip away.

We thought ourselves safe, but our stepmother discovered our hiding place. She had woven six shirts full of spells. She waited behind the castle wall. When we appeared, she threw the shirts into the wind. One flew over each of my brothers, transforming them into six great swans!

Stepmother turned to me. "Where is your sharp tongue now, sweet Sophie," she mocked. "If you want your brothers back then listen. Make six shirts—from the thorny thistle, sharp and cruel like your words. If you speak one word before the shirts are complete, your brothers will be swans forever!"

Fearful but determined, I flew from her to find my brothers.

For months I wandered.
One evening, I heard a rush of wings. Six beautiful swans touched the earth. My brothers stood before me!

"Dearest Sophie!" the eldest exclaimed. "We are allowed for one night to be with you in our true forms!" We chattered, laughed, and cried the whole night through.

"Come!" they said, as morning dawned. "We will take you where you can begin your task."

My brother swans set me down on the shore of a lake. There I built a small hut. Carefully cutting thistles that grew nearby, I spun and wove them into cloth. Finally, I began to sew the first shirt. I ignored the thorns that stabbed and stung, for I had to save my brothers.

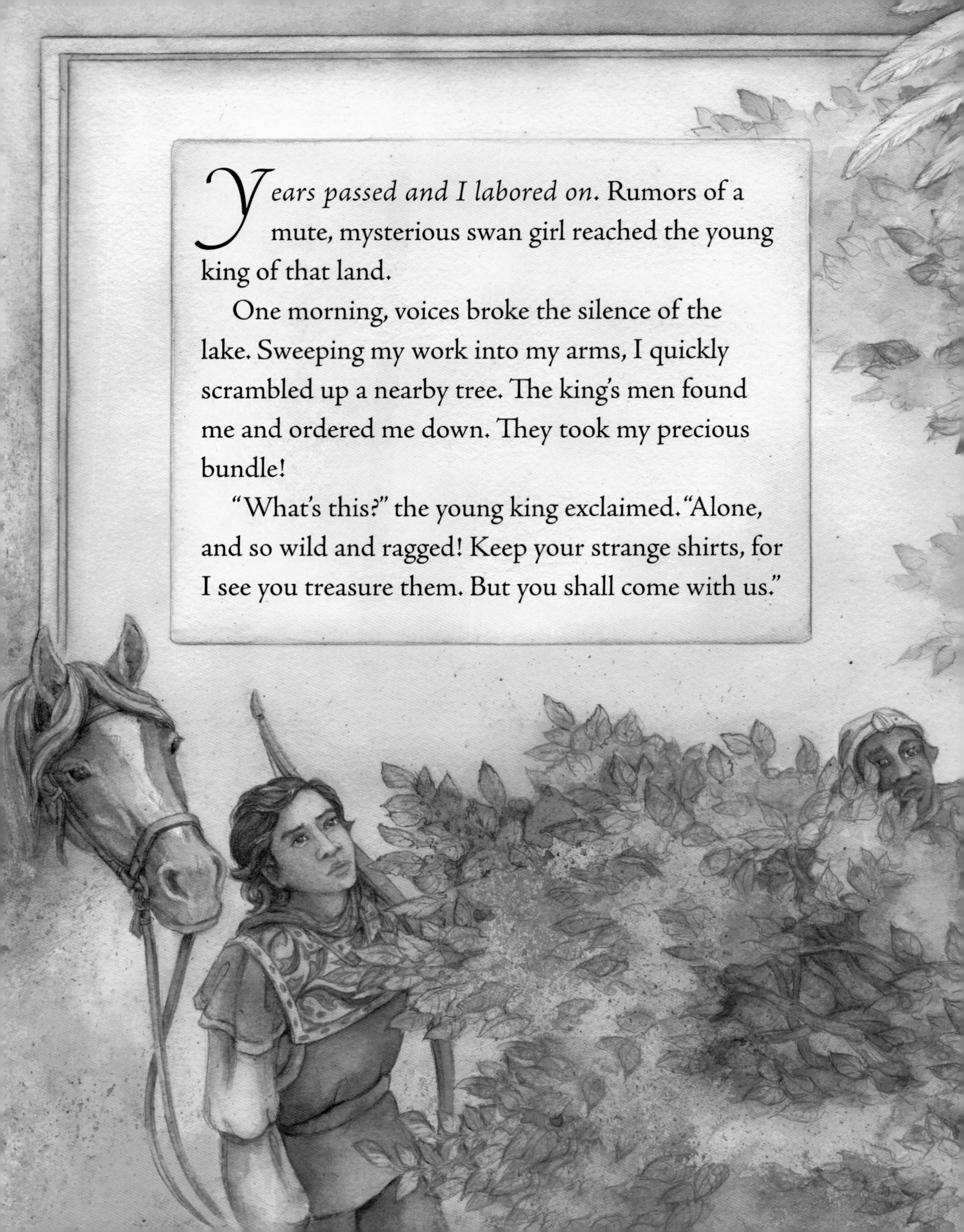

Years passed and I labored on. Rumors of a mute, mysterious swan girl reached the young king of that land.

One morning, voices broke the silence of the lake. Sweeping my work into my arms, I quickly scrambled up a nearby tree. The king's men found me and ordered me down. They took my precious bundle!

"What's this?" the young king exclaimed. "Alone, and so wild and ragged! Keep your strange shirts, for I see you treasure them. But you shall come with us."

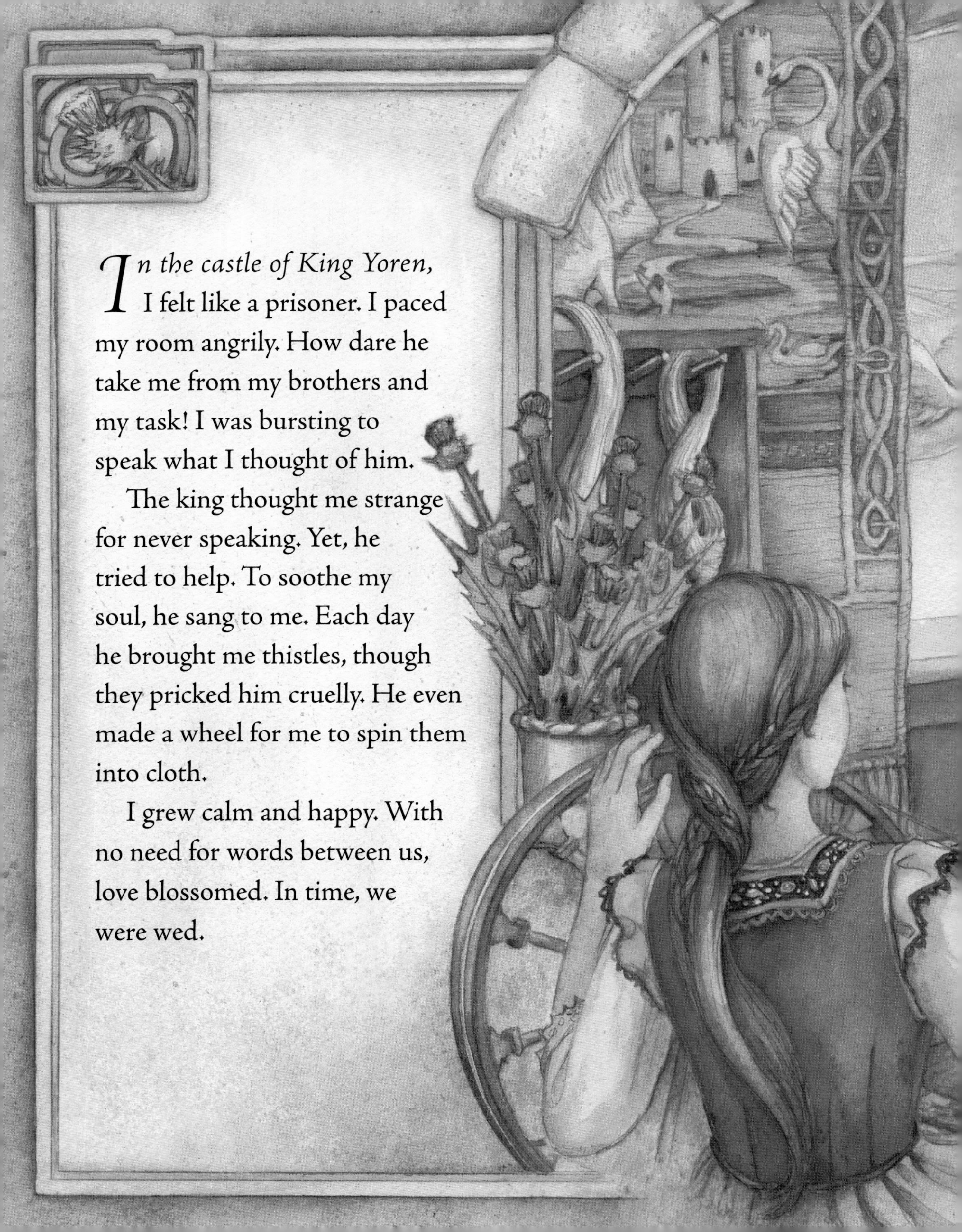

In the castle of King Yoren, I felt like a prisoner. I paced my room angrily. How dare he take me from my brothers and my task! I was bursting to speak what I thought of him.

The king thought me strange for never speaking. Yet, he tried to help. To soothe my soul, he sang to me. Each day he brought me thistles, though they pricked him cruelly. He even made a wheel for me to spin them into cloth.

I grew calm and happy. With no need for words between us, love blossomed. In time, we were wed.

What joy I felt when our daughter was born and the last shirt was nearly done! Then, without warning, my stepmother appeared. She put the castle to sleep and stole our little one away. Since I dared not speak my grief, many in the village thought the theft a wicked trick of mine.

With the shirts clutched to me, I was taken to the square to be tried for witchcraft. My own husband, the king, would be the judge!

The townsfolk cried, "Her silence is proof of her guilt." Still I would not speak. If I did, my brothers would remain swans forever!

Just then I heard the rush of wings. I threw the shirts high. My brothers flew into them.

Standing before us all were six beautiful young men, freed from our stepmother's spell at last! The youngest stood, yet with one white wing, the last sleeve unfinished.

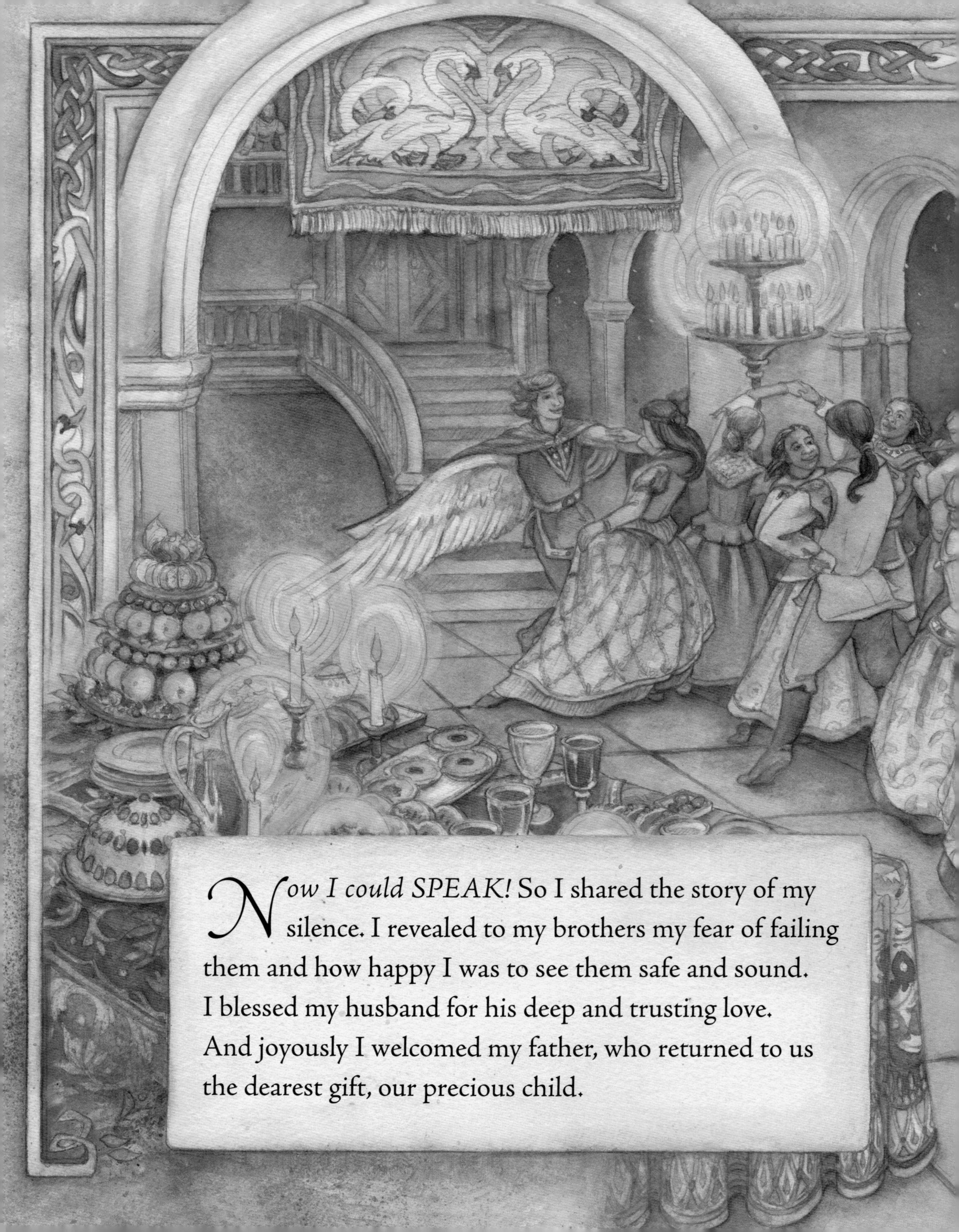

Now I could SPEAK! So I shared the story of my silence. I revealed to my brothers my fear of failing them and how happy I was to see them safe and sound. I blessed my husband for his deep and trusting love. And joyously I welcomed my father, who returned to us the dearest gift, our precious child.

Of my stepmother, I can tell you it was her own spell that brought her end. When I broke it, the thread of her life was cut. Though the spell was her curse, it was my blessing. I discovered what determination and love can do. I learned the vast power of words. And, I found the beauty in silence that stills our thoughts and lets us hear the flight of birds.

Author's Note

Legends of six-brothers-turned-into-swans were told by firesides long before Wilhelm and Jacob Grimm wrote one into their book of fairytales over 200 years ago. This story of a spirited girl who saves her brothers was my childhood favorite. Like most children, I wanted to know why things happened the way they did—especially in stories. I wanted to know why the brothers were changed into swans, why their sister had to save them, why she stayed silent. I wrote this version of the story so you, dear reader, could have the answers.

Heraldry and Swans

Long ago, people lived close to nature in small tribal bands, hunting and gathering nuts and berries to survive. These early people had great respect for animals they encountered in the wild. They often chose an animal with a specific characteristic ("strong" as a bear, "ferocious" as a lion) to represent a personal, family, or tribal trait.

In Sophie's time of kings and queens, her noble family would have a "coat of arms." This was a unique design of the family's special animal symbol, their colors, and their motto—a few words that inspired and guided them. It helped hold families together and identified one family from another. This coat of arms was painted onto the front of a wooden, leather, or metal protective shield used in battle, sewn onto a coat or tunic worn over armor, and displayed on large shields hung in the great hall of castles.

I chose a swan (known for its loyalty and strength) as the animal-symbol for Sophie's family. The word "swan," from the ancient word *swen,* means "to sound" or "to sing." The swans in my tale are so-called mute swans (*cygnus olor*); unlike the loud calls of other swans, they can make only soft sounds. Swans mate for life and defend their home territory fiercely, just as Sophie defends her mother's memory and resolves to reunite her family despite all the challenges set before her, including never to speak, even in her own defense.